HOLLY'S WISH

USA Today Bestselling Author
KATHLEEN LAWLESS

Cover Art Copyright Black Widow Books
ISBN 978-989873-19-9
Print ISBN 978-1-989873-71-7

TABLE OF CONTENTS

ABOUT HOLLY'S WISH

Do wishes come true?

All her life, Holly has believed in the power of wishing. Except for the "big one". The phone call that never came after a memorable encounter one Christmas Eve.

She can't forget Nico and their synchronicity that night.

Dare she risk a second heartbreak when her latest wish brings Nico back into her life?

DEDICATION

Holly's Wish is dedicated to my daughter, Reyna, for all her brainstorming help and feedback.

Chapter 1

Five days before Christmas…

Nicholas stared in dismay at the seven-foot-tall, fir Christmas tree in his sister's living room. The twins were asleep upstairs, and Sherry planned to surprise them by having the tree completely decorated by the time they woke up.

"It's easier without them helping," Sherry said as she passed him a box of colored balls, each one wrapped in protective tissue. "You should hang these. They're the ones you sent Mom every year." She shot him a pointed look. "She treasured them because they came from you. You should have seen her face every Christmas morning when she unwrapped the latest one and hung it on the tree."

Nicholas swallowed the taste of guilt. "I should have made more of an effort to get here to see her."

"Yes, you should have," Sherry said.

They continued their task in silence for a few minutes. How long had it been, Nic wondered, since he had last trimmed a tree? He looked over at

Sherry and marveled at everything she did. A thriving practice in natural medicine, three-and-a-half-year-old twins, and her husband deployed on the other side of the world. Trying to come up with an excuse not to spend Christmas with her and the nephews he'd never met hadn't been an option.

"I can't believe you took the entire week off," Sherry said. "Is that what happens once you make partner? Some poor office slave burns the candle at both ends so you look good in court?"

Nicholas grunted. He'd worked hard to make partner in just over five years, but he was beginning to realize he'd missed out on a lot.

Balanced on Sherry's stepladder, he hung the final decoration but must have misjudged the branch, for the bright red ball hit the ground, bounced on the carpet, and rolled behind an easy chair. As Nic retrieved the ornament and started up the ladder, he saw what looked like a New York phone number written in black ink, faded over the years, on the underside of the bright red ball.

"Did our mother have a secret admirer?" he

asked. "This one has a phone number written on it."

Sherry took the ball from his hand and turned it over, frowning. "I never noticed that before. It's one of the ones you sent her." She handed it back. "Speaking of decorations, I hope you're not planning to let that tradition die with Mom."

"Of course not," Nic said quickly. "But you have to wait for Christmas morning." He'd seen a Christmas shop on Main Street on his way here. He'd head there tomorrow and pick up a decoration for Sherry. He might as well get a couple for the twins while he was at it. If he started them young, they'd have enough baubles to decorate their own trees one day.

* * *

Holly trudged down Main Street, lugging her heavy bag of camera equipment from her latest shoot. Why did clients leave it till the last minute to decide they needed a family photo to include with their Christmas cards? As if this time of year wasn't busy enough.

She pushed open the door to the Dickens'

3

famous Gift Emporium, currently all done up for Christmas. "Hey! Kris," she called. "It's Holly. Are you out back?"

Kris Kringle, a retired actress of a certain age, with a staggering collection of stage costumes that she wore to the shop, strolled from the back room, wiping crumbs from the corner of her mouth. Today, she wore a Santa's elf costume, with green tights and a short red skirt that showed she still had great legs.

Holly grinned. "I didn't mean to interrupt your snack. I just need that list of families and gifts so I can start wrapping up the donated items."

"Here it is." Kris rummaged in her apron pocket and passed Holly the list of local families who had it tougher than usual this time of year and needed a little extra help. Her eyes twinkled behind wireless glasses that Holly knew were just for show. "I'm so glad you started Holly's Toy Chest to collect and distribute donations. Any plans for the holidays?"

Holly shrugged. "I'll spend the big day with

Sherry and her boys. Her hubby's overseas."

"Isn't it high time you had your own wedding and family, instead of photographing other people's?"

"How many times have you been married?" Holly shot back

"That's different," Kris said.

"I'm very happy with my life," Holly said.

"And a darn good photographer," Kris said. "You have a real gift of capturing the inner soul of the person you're taking the picture of."

Holly smiled indulgently. "I should take *your* picture one day."

"I think I'll keep my secrets, thank you."

It was impossible to tell how old Kris was, for she always dressed in costume and assumed a different identity on a revolving basis. Santa or his helper at Christmas, Cupid at Valentine's, Mrs. Easter Bunny during that time of year, and when there were no special holidays, favored her getup as a gypsy fortune teller.

Kris Kringle, obviously her stage name,

claimed that one day she'd had enough of Broadway's bright lights and moved here. Through the years, she came to know everyone who lived in Dickens.

"You should never underestimate the power of wishing," Kris said. "It always worked for me."

"I'm the queen of wishing," Holly said blithely. "Every shooting star, new moon, and birthday candle. You name it, I send my wish out there. It's not my fault no one seems to be listening."

"Your time will come," Kris said.

"Right now, I need to go edit these photos and email them to the last-minute clients, then get started on the wrapping. You have a good day."

"You too."

As Kris spoke, the shop door opened with a tinkle of overhead bells. Holly looked over to see a tall, dark haired man stamping snow off his feet, then took another look because, truthfully, there weren't a lot of good-looking men in Dickens.

Something about the newcomer seemed familiar, but before Holly could get a second look, he turned away. She was left with an impression of a square jaw and pronounced cheekbones, with a straight, masculine nose nicely balanced above full lips. Perhaps she photographed him at some point in the past.

When he passed her in the aisle without a second glance, she figured she must be mistaken. She paused at the door for one last glimpse, but his back was toward her. Typical man, doing his Christmas shopping at the last minute.

Holly stopped by Dickens's newspaper office on her way home. Print newspapers were getting to be a thing of the past in today's online world but Burt, the publisher, stubbornly clung to the old ways, and the townsfolks supported him with subscriptions and advertising. She had to drop off the latest "wish list" for Holly's Toy Chest in person because she knew Burt avoided reading his email.

"This is the last of the requests, Burt," she told him.

Burt switched his reading glasses from the top

of his head to the bridge of his nose and squinted at her list, which she had written in large print.

"How come youngsters these days want electronic gadgets instead of books and dolls and trainsets, like when I was their age?"

"Don't kid yourself," Holly said. "They still like toys."

"You taking the haul with you today?"

"I'll wait a few more days," Holly said. "Then I'll come by with the van."

"Folks are digging deep, same as always," Burt said.

Holly knew Burt would top up any unfulfilled requests, the way he always did. "That's why I love this town," she said. "Now I've got a date with the computer."

"You need to have yourself a real date, pretty young thing like you."

"If only you didn't have all girls," Holly said. It was their ongoing quip. She insisted she was waiting for someone just like Burt. Someone with old fashioned chivalry.

"Managed to get them all married off," Burt mumbled. "Cost me a king's ransom."

"Their dowries?" Holly teased.

"Worse," Burt said. "Those big fancy weddings they all wanted. You should know. You took the photos."

"You were the proudest father of the bride I ever saw. And the most handsome." Holly hitched her camera bag higher on her shoulder. "See you in a couple of days."

Even though dusk fell early these days, the streets were cheery, with Christmas lights on all the downtown buildings and glowing warmly through the windows.

Candy canes and wreaths adorned the streetlights. A star twinkled atop the huge, lit-up tree in the town square. Holly scuffed through the snow. She loved Christmas, even if it sometimes felt a little lonely.

* * *

Back in the gift shop, Nicholas was overwhelmed by the collection of Christmas ornaments. Macy's, where he usually shopped in New York, was never cluttered like this. Some of the decorations looked older than the woman dressed like an elf, who watched him with a speculative gaze. Maybe she worried every stranger was a shoplifter. He acknowledged her with a lift of his brow.

After ten minutes of prowling the aisles, trying not to knock anything over, he approached where she stood behind the till, shaking a snow globe.

"You have quite the selection," he told her.

"Something for everyone," the elf said.

"My sister has twin boys. I thought maybe wooden toy soldiers for the tree. Something they can also play with that's not too fragile."

She nodded sagely. "Always a wise choice. They're over this way."

"I need something for my sister as well. I used to buy my mother an ornament each year and now that she's gone, I'll transfer that tradition to my sister."

"Traditions are good to hold onto," the elf said.

He noticed she wore a great many rings on both hands.

"Are rings your tradition?" he asked.

She looked down at her hands and nodded. "I bought myself a good luck ring for every opening night."

So the elf had once been an actress. That explained a lot.

Nic pointed. "I think I'll take that glass slipper for my sister. She used to love Cinderella when she was a girl." Funny, he hadn't thought about that in years.

"And those two soldiers." One carried a trumpet, the other a drum, so the boys could tell them apart.

The woman's rings flashed brightly, reflecting light from the shop's many strings of Christmas lights that adorned the artificial trees on display, and wound through the overhead beams as she wrapped each ornament lovingly in tissue, almost as if she was parting with them reluctantly. She tucked all three into a paper bag that was stamped with holly leaves.

Holly! he thought. Why did the sight of printed holly leaves seem significant?

As he reached for his wallet, he paused. On a miniature tree near the till, a small silver angel twirled, her robe reflecting a rainbow of lights. Nic reached toward it for a closer look, then pulled his hand back as the edge of the ornament pricked his finger.

The elf didn't miss a beat, and lifted the angel from the tree. "She's a beauty, isn't she?" She placed the angel in Nic's palm. "So exquisitely made."

As Nic held the angel, he felt heat radiate through his hand and spark up his arm. The ornament must be hot from being so near the lights. The second he passed it back, his hand felt empty. "I'll take her as well," he said impulsively.

"Excellent choice," the woman said, before she wrapped the angel and added it to the bag with Nic's other purchases. "It's always good to follow your impulses."

Nic left the store shaking his head, unsure what had come over him. He wasn't impulsive by nature. Not anymore.

Chapter 2

Holly got up from her computer and stretched gratefully. The photos were edited and emailed to the client in time to be printed on their glossy printer and tucked into their friends' Christmas cards. Thank goodness some people still sent old-fashioned cards.

Holly remembered the excitement of the December mail deliveries when she was young. The fat stack of cards her mother would open and read to her and her sister, explaining who the people were and how she knew them, before she fashioned the colorful cards into garlands to hang in the apartment windows.

Her mother loved Christmas, but detested the cold. As soon as Holly and her sister, Ivy, were in college, their mother moved to the Caribbean where she met a sailor. These days the two of them spent their time sailing from tropical island to tropical island, and the closest thing to a Christmas card that Holly got from her mother was an email.

She stooped to plug in the lights on her Christmas tree. The tree was less than two feet high, a live pine that made the whole house smell good. Kris always managed to find miniature decorations for Holly's tree, and adding to them each year was a tradition she wouldn't miss out on. She reached to admire her newest addition, only to get a poke in her finger from a particularly sharp pine needle.

"Ouch!" She pulled her hand back and quickly made a wish, a childhood holdover from her favorite Christmas storybook.

The sudden movement must have jostled the tree, for it started to shift. The top branch swayed, toppling the fragile glass star to the wood floor where it shattered into a million irreparable pieces. Holly stared down at the wreckage then went to get the vacuum. She'd loved that star. Kris had come across it in the store's attic and insisted on giving it to her for her tiny tree.

She almost made it to the closet for the vacuum before the phone rang; her friend, Sherry.

"Just checking in about Christmas day," Sherry

said.

"Am I still invited?" Holly teased.

"Of course. I just wanted to warn you. My brother is here for the holiday."

"The pompous dick of a lawyer? The one who never came to visit your mother before she died, and still hasn't met the twins?"

"The same," Sherry whispered.

"Did hell freeze over?" Holly asked.

There was silence on the other end before Sherry spoke. "I'm sorry I told you so much about him. Now you have a preconceived notion before you even meet him."

"You've got that right," Holly said.

Sherry exhaled heavily. "Try not to let what I told you about him influence you when you two meet, okay? I might have been a bit harsh in my judgement. He's really not so bad. He's been a godsend, helping keep the twins amused."

"Are you into the rum and eggnog already?" Holly asked.

"Seriously," Sherry said. "Give him a chance."

"A chance for what?" Holly asked herself as she ended the call, already starting to regret that she'd agreed to spend Christmas day there. But Ivy was off to some glamorous ski town to meet her boyfriend's family. Once Holly finished delivering the surprise parcels to the families in need, sitting around by herself on Christmas day didn't hold much appeal.

* * *

Two days before Christmas...

Nic watched the twins fly past the Christmas tree, ornaments shaking in the breeze of their tail wind. They'd been like this ever since the tree went up.

Excited as all get out, running through the house in circles, and even though Sherry insisted they were too young to really understand about Christmas, Nic wasn't convinced.

Seeing the steadily growing mound of gifts under the tree reminded him that he'd better wrap the ornaments he bought the other day and add them to the pile. And figure out what to do with that silver angel he'd purchased.

"Have you ever been in that shop on Main Street? The Gift Emporium, I think it's called," Nic asked his sister.

"I haven't been there since before the twins were born. I didn't dare venture in when I was pregnant, my big belly would have knocked something over for sure. These days, I shudder to think what havoc the twins would wreak if I took them in. Is it still stuffed to the rafters?"

"Pretty much," Nic said.

"Was Kris Kringle there?" Sherry said. "Dramatic gal of indeterminate age?"

"Sounds like her. She was dressed like an elf." He shot her a look. "That can't be her real name."

"She used to be on Broadway. I think that was her professional name. She's a lot of fun."

Eccentric would have been his assessment.

"I picked up a little something for the tree." As Nic reached in the bag to pull out the angel, the darn thing pricked his finger again. He passed the angel to Sherry. "Careful. She has a habit of poking me."

Sherry took it from him. "Your hands are just too big for something so delicate." She turned it over. "Pretty. But it's too small for this tree. It would disappear on here." She passed it back.

"Yeah, you're right," Nic said, feeling silly. "I'm not even sure why I bought it."

"I know." Sherry snapped her fingers. "You should donate it to Holly's Toy Chest. My friend collects gifts for families in need. Someone with a small tree will love this."

Nic shot her a look. "You have a friend named Holly?"

Sherry rolled her eyes. Come to think of it, she'd been doing that a lot since he arrived.

"Holly's a photographer. She took that picture of the twins that I sent you after they were born."

"Here." Nic thrust the angel toward her. "She's your friend. You give it to her."

"Uh huh." Sherry shook her head. "It's time you got in the Christmas spirit. Drop this off at Holly's and I bet you'll feel really good after."

"I always donate to a worthy cause at

Christmas," Nic said defensively.

"Don't you mean you write a check? It's hardly the same thing as a hands-on donation to a worthy cause."

Nic looked down at the silver angel in his palm. Like in the shop earlier, it felt strangely warm. Shouldn't silver-colored metal be cold to the touch? "Where does your friend live?"

"She's across town in the storybook section. 123 Holly and Ivy Lane. You would have passed by there on your way from the airport."

Nic raised a brow. "You're kidding? Your friend Holly lives on Holly and Ivy Lane?"

"She said the name reminds her of her favorite Christmas story from when she was young."

"And that's why she moved there?" Nic shook his head at the gullibility of some people. "Can I borrow your car?"

"Not a chance," Sherry said. "How long since you drove a car in the snow, big brother? The walk will do you good."

"Hmmph," was all Nic said, as he shrugged

into his heavy wool jacket and tucked the angel gingerly into his pocket.

"I'll call her and w—tell her you're on your way."

Nic shot Sherry one last look before he left. Was that a speculative gleam in her eye?

"Anything you plan to warn—I mean tell me about her? Does she prick unexpected guests the way this angel keeps pricking me?"

"Be nice," Sherry said. "Show her your charming side. I know it's buried under there someplace."

Dickens was a cute town, Nic had to admit, as he cut across the Commons, the town square where a shiny white gazebo was all decked out in greenery and lights. There was a group of carolers off to one side, surrounded by a cluster of townspeople of every age; from seniors huddled on a bench to women pushing baby buggies. A few snowflakes rested on the shoulder of a life size statue near the middle of the square.

As he rounded the gazebo, a snowball hit him

in the face, followed by a spate of giggles. Smiling, he wiped the snow from his face. When was the last time he'd been hit by a snowball? Or the last time he'd thrown one?

He reached down, picked up a handful of snow, packed it into a ball the size of a softball and sent it toward the evergreen bush where the giggles had come from. There was an answering volley, and he responded with a second and a third snowball before he threw up his hands.

"I surrender, guys."

"Why?" came a prepubescent voice.

"I know when I'm outnumbered, that's why."

Across from the Commons, he passed an old-fashioned horse-drawn sleigh and driver.

"Need a ride?" the driver asked.

"Not tonight," Nic said. "But can I hire you for tomorrow afternoon?" What a great surprise for Sherry and the boys.

He continued on his way and soon found Holly and Ivy Lane. 123 radiated a warm coziness, with smoke rising from the chimney, lights shining from the front window, and a lighted wreath on the door. He lifted the knocker and winced when something, probably a piece of holly, pricked his finger.

Through his pocket, he could feel the warmth radiated by the Silver Angel.

Chapter 3

Holly answered the door seconds after someone knocked. Her eyes widened as the porch light illuminated the features of the man standing there. She gripped the edge of the door for support.

"You must be Holly," the man said with a familiar, engaging smile. "I'm Nic."

Holly couldn't believe her eyes! The man affectionately dubbed by Sherry as "Nic the dick," was in actual fact, Nico.

Whoever originally said, "careful what you wish for," hadn't been kidding.

Holly's heart raced as she stepped back, opening the door wide. "Please come in. Sherry said you have a donation."

She waited while he wiped his wet boots, then led him into the living room and turned to face him. Despite the fact that he'd brushed by her quickly in the Emporium, she knew why she had felt that unmistakable flash of recognition.

Would he recognize *her*? She raised a hand to

her shoulder length rainbow-hued hair. Born a blonde, she was always playing with the color, which had been jet black and long when she and Nico had first met. Her hair had been straight then as well, unlike its current tangle of curls. What else was different? Her makeup was far more subtle, and she'd finally grown into her features which used to feel too big for her face. Or so said her critical photographer's eye.

But he wasn't looking her way.

"Cute tree," Nico said. Given his height and broad shoulders, her tree looked almost like a toy. "Sherry's is a monster. I needed a ladder to put the star on top. Speaking of stars..." He reached into his jacket pocket and pulled out the angel. "I have a donation for your charity."

He paused midway of handing it to her, and seemed to really look at her for the first time. "Have we met before?"

Holly held her breath, waiting...

"I know," Nico said. "I saw you earlier this week in that crazy shop where I got this." He winced. "Be careful with it. The darn thing keeps poking me."

"You make it sound vicious? Is that why you're donating it?"

"I thought it was a nice idea," Nico said. He sounded wounded. She hoped he felt as wounded as she had for months, waiting for the phone to ring, waiting for his call. He'd told her his name was Nico.

She'd thought that night had meant something to him, the way it had meant something to her. But he'd never called.

She exhaled. She couldn't believe he was here, in her house.

Never in her wildest imaginings had she linked Nico, from that magic Christmas Eve in New York, to Sherry's lawyer brother, Nicholas.

She noticed he still held the angel as he continued to look at her as if seeing her for the first time.

"Would you like to sit down?" she said finally. He looked a little dazed.

"Thanks." He grabbed the nearest chair. "What exactly is your charity?"

Holly waved her arm in the direction of a mountainous stack of Christmas gifts in one corner, some wrapped, others waiting to be transformed, designed to delight a special youngster on Christmas day as they ripped off the fancy wrap. "I collect and wrap donated gifts to distribute on Christmas Eve to households who need a little extra help this time of year."

Nico actually looked shocked. "How do you know what people need?"

"Kris, from the Emporium, helps me. I'm not sure if she has a sixth sense or an inside track, but she's never wrong. I tell the donors what's needed and they shop for it. A lot of people don't have kids to buy for anymore. They enjoy it."

"And you distribute these gifts all over town on Christmas Eve? Do you climb down the chimney, too?"

Holly shook her head. "The parents know to expect me. Once the kids are in bed, they leave the door unlocked."

"You wouldn't find that happening in New York," Nico said.

"It's different here," Holly replied.

"I'll say."

Holly noticed he no longer seemed so anxious to pass over the silver angel. In fact, he was starting to look relaxed. She could almost see the stress melt, the same way she had that night at Rockefeller Center.

"Drat!" he said suddenly, staring at the angel. "This thing must hate me. I've lost count of how many times it's stabbed me tonight."

"They say everything happens for a reason," Holly said. She still hadn't sat down. She didn't want Nico getting too comfortable, like—she had to stop thinking about that night. For a while there, she'd almost convinced herself he had been a figment of her lonely imagination. Now she knew he was real.

And too self-centered to remember the girl he ran into, literally, that night they'd both been alone on Christmas Eve, skating at Rockefeller Center. At the time she'd thought their meeting was serendipitous, for that entire evening had been like something from a dream. Or a romantic novel. Girl on her own runs into handsome man who also happens to be alone for the holidays, the connection between them nothing short of magical.

"I know!" He stood up suddenly, taller and broader than she remembered. "You don't have a star on the top of your tree. This angel will be perfect."

Before she could stop him, he'd crossed the room and placed the angel on the bare tree top. He took a step back and cocked his head to study it. "That looks better."

Her heart started to gallop. She felt dizzy. What was happening? It was her turn to sink down into the nearest chair. Something about the angel, about Nico being here, placing it on her tree—she felt like she was flashing back in time. The two of them. A short, scrawny tree. A tiny room with a fire crackling. But that's not what she recalled from that night. Her tiny New York apartment had had no tree or blazing fireplace.

"Are you okay?" He hunkered down next to her, his hand resting on the arm of her chair, touchably close.

"Sorry. Just—Yeah, I'm fine. It was a hectic day."

Nico stood and swiped his hair back from his face with one hand in the endearing way she remembered. He started toward the door, then turned. "Hey! Need some help tomorrow night? With your deliveries?"

"That's not—"

"Please," he said in that persuasive way that she hadn't been able to say no to. "Sherry accused me of being a bit of a Scrooge, and she's right. I let work take over my life for too many years. It's time I did something for others."

"Dickens is not a place to come and put on your Santa hat for a few hours to make yourself feel better," Holly said stonily.

Nico swallowed thickly, his eyes darkly

intense, drawing her in. "I see my reputation has preceded me. I expect Sherry's said a few choice things over the years about her self-centered big brother, and I can't even defend myself. Everything she said is true."

She opened her mouth to tell him she didn't need his help, but somehow the exact opposite message flew past her lips. It was as if someone else was controlling her vocal cords, accepting his offer to help her deliver the gifts.

She could tell from his pleasantly surprised expression that he'd been expecting her refusal.

"That's great. Do you need a hand with the wrapping? I'm really good at putting my thumb down to hold the ribbon while it's being tied."

"That's all you're good at," Holly said. "You're all thumbs when it comes to folding corners because your hands are too big." She bit her lip abruptly.

Nico gave her a funny look. "How did you know that?"

"Sherry told me," she said quickly.

He continued to eye her closely.

She couldn't let him help her. If she spent too much time in his company, sooner or later she was bound to say or do something that would twig his memory as to who she was, and *that* would be awkward.

"Seriously, I've been doing this on my own for years. I've got my routine down pat. You'd only be in the way."

He acted like he didn't hear her as he crossed the room to the mantle and picked up a framed photo she had taken last year of the commons and the decorated tree.

"Sherry said you're a photographer. Is this your work?"

She nodded.

"You're not half bad," he said.

"Gee, thanks," she drawled sarcastically.

He set the photo back down. "Sherry said you're coming for Christmas dinner. Can I hire you to take some photos of Sherry and the kids while you're there? She can email them to Josh."

Holly shook her head. "I never work on

Christmas Day. Besides, the family will be Facetiming that day." Already, she was wondering what kind of emergency she could invent to get her out of dinner with Sherry and Nico.

"Can I buy a gift certificate then? For a family portrait once Josh gets home?"

"I suppose," Holly said reluctantly.

"I'd need it now," Nico said when she didn't move. "That way I can put it in Sherry's stocking."

"Oh." Holly rose. "Sure. I'll print you something on the computer." She wasn't sure how it happened, one minute she was crossing the room, the next minute her foot became tangled in the throw rug in front of the fireplace and she was going down. Nico tried to break her fall, just as he had years earlier on the skating rink. And just like then, the two of them landed in a tangle of limbs.

Chapter 4

Nic pushed himself to one elbow and stared down at the woman on the floor beneath him. Her eyes were closed and her lids were fluttering as her chest rose and fell with each indrawn breath.

Nic blinked. Something shadowy hovered behind the thin veil of his memory, something he felt it was important he remember, but try as he might, the fragment eluded him.

Holly's eyes flew open. She looked up at him and her mouth made a round O of surprise.

"You okay?" Nic asked as he pushed himself to his feet and stretched out a hand to help her up.

Holly nodded and looked around, as if seeking a different means to reach her feet then, reluctantly it seemed, placed her hand in his. She hardly weighed a thing and the force of his overzealous tug on her arm sent her careening into him, which didn't feel like a bad thing at all. She fit nicely against him, and he was enjoying the feel of her soft, womanly curves before she let go and stepped away, only to let out a yelp and crumple to the floor.

Nic crouched at her side. "What's wrong?"

"My ankle. I must have sprained it when I fell."

"We should go to the hospital. Make sure it's not broken."

"I know a sprain when I feel one." Holly half crawled, half bum-walked over to the couch and pulled herself onto it. She stretched her leg onto the coffee table and peeled back her thick sock to examine her ankle. "Definitely sprained," she said ruefully.

Nic leapt to action. "I'll get you ice." He started toward a door he assumed led to the kitchen, then stopped. "Do you have ice?"

"There's a cold pack in the freezer."

The ice pack was easy to find as there wasn't much in her freezer besides a couple of frozen one-person dinners, half a loaf of sliced bread, and a lone bag of berries. The single life. It reminded him of his freezer in the city, minus the berries.

The kitchen was compact and tidy, with a

couple of plates and some cutlery drying in a rack above the sink. He grabbed a dish towel from the handle of the oven and wrapped it around the ice pack.

Holly was right where he had left her, staring balefully at her rapidly swelling ankle.

"Thanks." She took the ice and positioned it on her ankle, then sucked in her breath.

"Do you have any pain meds I can get you?" Nic asked. He wasn't used to feeling so helpless.

Holly shook her head then rested it against the sofa back. Nic watched her, wondering why he felt so drawn to his sister's friend. Normally he'd be beating a hasty retreat by now; instead, he was shrugging out of his coat, reluctant to leave.

"Can I get you anything?" he asked. "A glass of water? A cup of tea?"

Holly studied him from beneath half-closed lids. Finally, she pointed to a wine rack in the corner. "I think I could use a glass of merlot. You're welcome to join me if you'd like."

Grateful to be useful, Nic found the wine, and

without asking, located the wine opener in the first kitchen drawer he opened. The wine glasses were in the first cupboard he looked in. Everything about Holly and her setup felt so darn familiar. He turned and stared through the doorway to where she sat on the sofa. He'd never been to Dickens, never been in Holly's house, and yet...

He poured two glasses of wine and carried them through to the living room, setting hers within easy reach. He wanted to make a toast, but toasting her sprained ankle didn't seem right.

"To Christmas," he finally said, raising his glass.

"To Christmas," Holly echoed. "My favorite time of the year."

"Why's that?"

"Our mother loved the season. We didn't have much growing up, but she always made it special. I guess it's ingrained."

"A lot of people dread it," Nic said.

"Including you?" Holly asked.

"Why would you say that?"

"This is your first time in a long time joining your family for the holidays." Straight from the hip.

"Work sounds like a pathetic excuse now that I'm here," he said. "At the time it seemed legitimate." He looked straight at her. "What made you start your holiday cause to distribute gifts?"

"I believe Christmas should be special for everyone, no matter what their circumstances. Plus, I figured out a long time ago that a lot of people feel better giving than receiving, so I'm providing an easy avenue."

"It has to be a lot of work for one person." Nic rose. "On that happy note, old ten thumbs is going to help you with the rest of the wrapping."

"No. Really—"

"You just sit there and nurse your ankle while you issue orders. "He flashed her a smile. "People don't get to boss me around very often, so keep it to yourself. No bragging to Sherry how I was doing your bidding all night. It might give her ideas."

* * *

Much as Holly hated to admit it, Nic's help was

a godsend. By the time he left, all the donated gifts were wrapped and organized, ready for Christmas Eve. The bottle of merlot was empty and her ankle was still sore, but she declined his teasing offer to help her into bed.

"What time tomorrow?" he asked as he put on his coat and gloves.

"Tomorrow?" she said.

"What time should I be here to help you load up your delivery van?"

Holly blew out a breath. The last thing she wanted was to spend a second Christmas Eve in the company of Nico, but the fates seemed to have other plans.

"I'll come early and bring a pizza," he offered.

"Oh, no I—"

"No arguments. I've seen inside your fridge," he said.

"I was leaving room for any leftovers Sherry sends me home with," Holly said.

Nico smiled. "There will still be room."

* * *

Nic's step was light as he cut through the commons and paused in front of the life-sized statue, wondering who she symbolized, for there was no plaque. As he walked through the still-bustling streets with the sound of Christmas carols filling the air, he had to admit Dickens was growing on him, even the quirky street names. Sherry lived in the resort area, on a street named Cayman Close.

The house was quiet, which meant the twins were in bed. Sherry sat before the lit-up tree with a book on her lap. "Everything okay?" she asked. "You were gone a long time."

"Your friend had a slight mishap," Nic said as he took off his coat. "She sprained her ankle, so I stayed and helped her wrap the rest of the gifts she's taking out tomorrow night."

"You did *what*?"

"You heard me," Nic said.

Sherry's brow furrowed slightly. "Then—I take it you two got along okay?"

"Uh huh," Nic said with only half of his attention, as he walked over to the tree. One red ball seemed to shimmer brighter than anything else around it, drawing him close. It had to be a reflection from the lights. As he approached, the ball swayed on the branch, even though there was no draft, and he realized it was the one with the writing on it.

He pulled over a stool and lifted it off the tree, then turned to Sherry. "Do you remember what year I sent this decoration to Mom?"

Sherry started to shake her head, then stopped. "I do remember. That's the one that showed up after Christmas because you mailed it late."

"Right." Nic nodded. "Work was a bugger that December and I didn't get a chance to shop until Christmas Eve." He turned the ball around in his hand. He'd met a girl that night after shopping. A night that had stretched into morning, two lonely people somehow connecting in one of the largest cities in North America.

"No names," she whispered in his ear when he asked. *"Just you and me alone together as Christmas day dawns."*

She'd laughed when he asked for her number. She told him it if serendipity was truly at work, he'd find where she'd written it, and to call her when he did.

"I'm Nico," he'd said as he left. "Just so you know who I am when I call."

She'd blown him a kiss as he closed the door behind him. "I'll be waiting."

He stared in disbelief at the number on the Christmas ball, then fumbled his phone from his pocket.

"What are you doing?" Sherry was watching him with a curious expression.

"This number," he said. "I need to see whose it is."

His shoulders sagged as a recorded message told him the number was no longer in service.

"What is it?" Sherry said when he put his phone away. "What's wrong?"

"Nothing," Nic said. "It wasn't meant to be."

Chapter 5

Christmas Eve day...

If her ankle wasn't so sore, Holly would have been pacing. She was always restless on Christmas Eve, following the build-up of the past month as she compiled the gift list and matched it to the donations. Her gaze strayed to the boxes of gifts, ready and waiting. She always went to the houses with the youngest children first, as houses with older kids were trickier. The teens might be in bed, but were they asleep? As far as she knew, in the five years she had been doing this, she'd never been seen.

Normally, she'd go for a run or something to work off this pent-up adrenalin. Adrenalin she tried hard to convince herself had nothing to do with Nico. Just like last time, it was hard to look around the room and not remember him—sitting there, standing there. His presence filled a room and lingered long after he left.

She tried to call her sister, but got voice mail.

Her in-box showed an email from her mother. Apparently, it was already Christmas day where her mom was, on a sailboat in some exotic place with a name Holly couldn't pronounce.

Holly flopped onto the couch and clicked on the TV. Maybe a holiday movie would help distract her. An hour and a half later she sighed and turned the TV off. The romantic Christmas movie had only made her feel worse. She stared up at the silver angel Nico had placed on her tree. If there really was magic, if wishes really came true...

Look where her wishes had landed her!

Just then, she heard a loud jingle of what sounded like sleigh bells outside. She rose and went to the window. Through the early dusk, she made out an old-fashioned horse-drawn sleigh outside her house. She half turned away from the sight of the happy family out for a sleigh ride, a mom, dad and two kids, until the man leapt out and started for her door.

Nico!

Sherry and the twins spotted her through the

window and waved for her to come out.

"What the—?" She limped to the door just as Nico was reaching for the knocker.

"Merry Christmas Eve!" he said.

Her heart climbed into her throat. Why did he have to look even more devastatingly handsome than by firelight?

"I figured you might be at loose ends and free to join us on a little spin around town."

"Oh, I—"

"You can't disappoint Sherry and the boys. Where's your coat?"

He brushed past her as if he had every right to be there, and reached for her winter coat on a hook near the door. "We've got heated blankets and a bottle of warm mulled wine that Sherry snuck aboard. Come on."

"I should be resting my ankle for later," she said stubbornly, even as she glanced longingly toward the street.

An old-fashioned sleigh ride. What fun! But dangerous. Time spent in Nico's company was a bad thing. Before she could catch her breath, he'd be back to his life in the city and she'd be left with her unfulfilled wishes.

"We're not taking no for an answer," Nico said. "I have orders to carry you out there myself, if it comes to that."

"I'm not sure I can get my boots on over my swollen ankle."

Nico was sticking her arms into her coat sleeves as if she was a child. "Then I'll just have to carry you." He grabbed her cashmere scarf and hat before he swept her up in his arms.

"Wait," Holly said. "I need my keys and my phone and—"

Nico scooped the two items, along with her gloves, from the side table in the entrance hall, checked that the door was locked, and started down the front walk with her in his arms.

Holly took a breath. The air was crisp and fresh, the dusk-tinged sky studded with a few wispy clouds.

"Whatever you do for a living, you must be

darn good at it," Holly said, resisting the urge to press her cheek to his neck. He smelled divine, a woodsy, spicy, masculine fragrance that was partly him and partly an exotic after shave.

"I'm a prosecuting attorney," he said. "And I never lose."

"Never?" Holly asked.

"Rarely," Nico amended. "If I lose, I appeal." He grinned. "Then I win."

Holly was breathless by the time they reached the sleigh. She told herself it was the fresh air, but the truth was it was being caught and held in Nico's arms. She studied him in the dim light and felt a throb of desire ripple through her. Her body definitely had a memory.

Nico settled her in the seat across from Sherry and the boys before he joined her, so close his shoulder brushed hers as he settled the blanket over both their laps. She felt his thigh rubbing against hers. Did he need to sit so close?

Sherry didn't seem to notice as she reached over to give her a hug. Next to their mom, the twins were bundled up in identical snowsuits and looked almost angelic.

"I knew Nic would talk you into joining us. Isn't this a fabulous idea? He totally surprised us with this early Christmas gift."

"Thanta cometh tonight," Robbie told her, with his endearing lisp. Will, the quieter of the two, nodded, wide-eyed.

Holly leaned forward. "Have you been good for your mom? Keeping your room clean and stuff like that?"

The twins looked at each other and burst out laughing.

Sherry rolled her eyes. "Not only that, Uncle Nic has been a very bad influence, getting them even more wound up." As the sleigh started up, she reached into a wicker basket at her feet.

"Can we have juice?" Will asked, watching his mom pour mulled wine into insulated mugs and pass one to Nico and Holly.

"I told you. This is adult juice. You get hot chocolate. But you have to be very careful not to spill." Both boys nodded solemnly as Sherry pulled out a second thermos.

"This is wonderful!" Holly pulled her hat on tight as the sleigh picked up speed. "Where are we going?"

"Just a little tour around to look at the lights."

Nico elbowed her gently beneath the blanket. "Because the boys aren't excited enough already."

Holly felt warm and toasty from the inside out as she sipped her mulled wine and listened to the chatter around her. Like that first night she met Nico, she no longer felt lonely.

The horse's hooves clopped quietly over the snowy streets as their sleigh wound through the storyland area, circled the Commons, then headed for Main Street, where the driver pulled over so they could listen to a group of carolers. A short distance from town stood Holly Hill Inn, all lit up and ready for Christmas.

Somehow, Nico's hand found its way to Holly's leg beneath the blanket and settled there, accelerating the heat pumping through her veins.

When he leaned close, he sent her a smile that took away her breath with the intimacy of it.

"I've missed this," Nico said. "There's something magical about Christmas Eve."

Holly used to think so, too, but these days she concentrated on making it magical for others.

Across from them, their tummies full of hot chocolate, the two boys eventually started to yawn. Sherry gave Nico a look. "I think it's time I get my guys home so they can hang up their stockings."

"Mom—" they both groaned in unison.

"See," Nico said with a wink, "my earlier strategy to tire them out worked."

"The sooner you go to sleep, the sooner Santa comes and it will be Christmas," Holly said.

When Nico leaned forward to speak to the driver, Holly instantly missed the warmth of his body pressed against hers.

After a brief exchange, Nico settled back next to her and the sleigh started off toward Sherry's. Holly straightened. "I should be dropped off first. I have stuff I need to do tonight."

Under the blanket, Nico's hand rested atop hers, his large fingers twined through her smaller ones. "It's okay, Holly. You don't need to do everything alone. You've got me to help."

By the time they reached Sherry's, both the boys were leaning sleepily against their mom.

Nico climbed gracefully from the sleigh. "I'll take them in," he said, and waited patiently as Sherry passed him one twin for each arm. He gave Holly a heated look. "I'll be right back."

Sherry picked up her wicker basket with the thermoses and cups. "That was fun. I haven't done anything so festive since before the twins were born."

Holly's heart pounded as she watched Nico stride toward the house with a youngster in each arm, as if he'd been doing it forever. Who knew he'd be a natural with young children?

She looked over to see Sherry watching her with a speculative expression, and shrugged. "He's not what I expected from your stories."

Sherry continued to give her the look.

"Suddenly, he seems like a different guy. I'm glad he's helping you tonight," she added.

"So am I," Holly said.

Chapter 6

Nic arrived back at the carriage in time to see Holly checking the time on her phone. "What time do you like to head out?"

"I try to have the van loaded by ten," she said.

"Good, we have time," Nic said.

"Time for what?" Holly asked.

"Time for a romantic sleigh ride, just the two of us. The twins are cute and all but—" He put his arm around her shoulder and pulled her close. As she snuggled against him, her delicate, rose-scented perfume teased his senses. He closed his eyes and savored the closeness, aware he'd smelled similar a similar scent a long time ago.

Abruptly Holly's stomach made an unladylike noise. She pulled away to face him.

"You might recall, someone promised me pizza."

Nic snapped his fingers. "I did. And I bet you think I forgot, didn't you?"

"You didn't forget?"

Nic leaned toward the driver. "What's our next destination?"

The driver looked over his shoulder as he answered. "Pizzaria Pantry."

Nic settled back smugly. "See? I didn't forget."

At the pizza place, Nic jumped out of the sleigh and hurried inside for his order. As he stood at the counter, he looked out the window to where Holly sat, bundled up and waiting. She saw him and flashed a smile that set his insides churning in a way that was both thrilling and foreign.

New York was full of interesting single women: professionals, models, and actresses that his lawyer friends were always trying to set him up with, but none of them affected him the way Holly did. She was real and grounded, generous and spontaneous, all at the same time. She took pictures of other people's happiest moments, and spent Christmas Eve enhancing the holiday for others.

"Here's your change, man," said the youth behind the counter.

"Keep it," Nic said. "Merry Christmas."

The young man's eyes widened. "Wow! Thanks!"

Nic gathered up the pizza box and a handful of napkins and hurried back to the waiting sleigh, reluctant to be away from Holly's side a second longer than necessary.

"Where are we going?" Holly asked, once they were underway.

Nic noticed Holly tucked into her pizza slice with gusto, another nice change from the actresses and models who barely picked at their food, insisting they weren't hungry.

"I told the driver, wherever he thinks, as long as we're back at your place by eight. That should be enough time, right?" It felt really important he not disrupt Holly's normal Christmas Eve schedule.

"That should work."

Nic sat back, contentment flowing through him as he gazed skyward and munched on his pizza. "The stars never look this bright in the city. I can see so many more of them."

"That was one of the first things I noticed when

I moved here," she said.

He straightened to face her. "Where did you live before?" For some reason he'd assumed she was a local. She stiffened, and withdrew the slightest bit from his side. His lawyer mind kicked into gear. Did she have a hidden past? Something in her background she didn't want people to know about?

Her face was in shadow, half-turned from him. "Like you, I hail from a big city," she said vaguely.

"Which city?" he asked.

"What am I? On the witness stand?" she countered.

She tried to make it sound teasing, but it seemed obvious she didn't want him to know where she was from.

"Not at all," he said, vowing to quiz Sherry in the morning and find out just how well she knew Holly.

* * *

Holly knew the exact the moment the energy between her and Nico shifted. She'd done it deliberately, remained vague about her background for a couple of reasons. For one, she didn't want to say or do anything that might trigger him to the fact that they'd met before. She also was starting to feel, just like last time, a little too cozy in his presence, as if she'd known him forever.

Her mind had started to conjure up future Christmas sleigh rides, little ones on their laps. Or was that past Christmas lives? Not that she believed in reincarnation, but the ease and familiarity she felt around Nico last time hadn't lessened over the years.

"What's the place ahead?" he asked.

"That's a B&B, Holly Hill Inn. The owner goes all out with the decorations every year."

"The house looks like something from the last century, transported into modern day," Nico said.

"I always felt that, too." A white picket fence surrounded a two-story residence, clad in red clapboard siding. Fresh white trim around the windows and doors was offset by traditional Christmas greenery, red ribbons, and hundreds of white lights. "We'll be coming by here later."

"We will?"

"I have a little something for some of their guests."

As they sat there, looking back toward town and drinking in the view, Holly felt that unmistakable something that had first drawn her to Nico. Almost of their own volition, her limbs softened and lost their rigidity, once more easing her closer to his side. Her heart rate increased as she slowly turned his way. Their eyes met and something inside her warmed and melted. She sighed softly, seconds before his lips found hers.

Everything about kissing Nico felt right. There was no awkward bumping of noses or clashing of teeth as their mouths met. Like before, she had the most uncanny sense of having come home, where she belonged, connected to this man on so many levels. Blood raced through her limbs, making her feel alive like never before, while his talented lips sipped, tasted, and nibbled hers.

She moaned softly in the back of her throat,

which he took as encouragement to deepen the kiss, to plough his fingers through her hair, nails grazing her scalp, all the while holding her as if he'd never let her go.

Except he had let her go.

Eventually they drew apart, looking deep into one another's eyes. Nico looked unsure about what had just happened, but Holly knew. There was no denying the feeling of rightness in their being together.

Like years earlier, she was the yin to his yang, about to share another Christmas Eve with him.

And like before, she didn't want to miss a second of it.

Vaguely she grew aware the sleigh had started moving, taking them down the hill and back to town.

And just like that, she was newly energized! It was Christmas Eve, and she had work to do.

Chapter 7

Thanks to copious sessions with her ice pack earlier in the day, the swelling of her ankle had receded and Holly was able to carefully put a little pressure on the injured limb, but she knew there was no way she could have made countless trips from the house to the van and back again with her arms full of packages.

Nico meticulously followed her instructions as the van was loaded, gifts slated for early delivery at the front, while the ones to be delivered later were stored toward the rear of the van.

At last, it was time to get started. Holly pulled out the map she had printed, marking the locations and addresses with a bright red sharpie, easy to read by the van's interior lights.

Nic grinned. "An old-fashioned girl? No GPS?"

Holly shot him a look. "Where would I be if my phone suddenly died? You can always count on paper."

"I agree," Nico said. "Technology is great, but

sometimes the old way is better. Do kids still write to Santa, or do they email him these days?"

"All I know is, most kids in grade school know a lot more about phones and computers than I do. And I still cherish getting paper cards in the mail."

"I'll drive," Nico said. "Just tell me where to turn and where to stop and I'll do the rest."

* * *

Nic had to hand it to Holly. What she had committed to was quite an undertaking. Not only did they slip silently into the unlocked homes, they had to make sure they didn't track in any snow, and that they locked each door behind them.

"Here, drink this," Holly whispered, handing him a glass of milk.

"I don't like milk," Nic said.

"Santa likes milk." Holly scooped the Christmas cookies from the plate by the fireplace, along with a carrot. "And you offered to help."

So he had. "My duties were not fully disclosed," he whispered back as he plugged his nose and tried not to gag on the room temperature milk, aware of Holly's silent laughter.

Outside, he helped her back into the van, his hands lingering at her waist. They'd been at this for almost two hours, with the van ringing nearly nonstop with their laughter. He couldn't remember the last time he'd laughed so much, or felt this carefree, even when he slipped on a patch of ice and almost did the limbo trying not to drop the gifts or land on his ass, all of which had sent Holly into fits of laughter. He enjoyed watching the way her face lit up with merriment and exaggerated his movements, just to set her off again.

"What do you do with all those cookies?" he asked. "And don't tell me you eat them. That's not even possible."

"I take them to the senior center on the other side of town. A lot of those people have no family and they enjoy homemade goodies, especially the lopsided ones the kids make."

Nic felt a rush of emotion, suddenly ashamed of the way he'd let work rule his life, missing out on those last golden years with his mother. She'd lived in the center Holly referred to. "Are there a lot of seniors with no families?" he asked, forcing the words past the sudden lump in his throat.

"The town has an 'adopt a grandparent' program for seniors who are alone. The seniors get a surrogate family and the children learn how to be kind to the elderly. It's a win-win."

"What a great idea."

"Your mother wasn't part of it because she had Sherry here, but the boys were little when she passed away. Once they're a bit older, I expect Sherry will adopt a new grandparent. Not to take your mother's place, of course," she added quickly. "No one could do that."

"I think she should," Nic said gruffly. "Where to next?"

"Last stop, Holly Hill Inn, where we were earlier. There are usually a few guests staying there on their own and Kat, the owner, likes to make sure everyone has something to open in the morning."

"It must really feel good, making a difference in other people's lives the way you do."

"I enjoy being involved," Holly said. "Christmas is about joy, yet some people find it a very difficult time."

"I don't mean just Christmas," Nic said. "You also capture some of their happiest moments in life, commemorate a memory so they have it forever."

"I don't make the memory," Holly said, "I just help preserve it." She slanted him a look. "It's not like I'm ridding the streets of criminals or whatever it is you do to uphold justice."

"I used to think what I did was really important," Nic said. "But there's a lot that goes on behind the scenes. Plea bargains. Leniency in exchange for damning testimony. One criminal will turn on another so fast your head would spin, and the bad guys don't always get locked up."

"Don't the good guys always win?" Holly said lightly.

"We try," Nic said. "No justice system is perfect."

Where had all this come from? He hadn't realized until this moment just how dissatisfied he'd been feeling lately. As he drove, he snuck a glance at Holly. She had a way of digging stuff out of him that he didn't know was in there. How did she do that? Almost as if she knew him better than he knew himself; or had known him a really long time.

He stopped the van in front of the B&B. "The outside lights are still on."

"I know." Holly pulled on her gloves as she spoke. Red, he noticed, just like her hat and scarf. Her coat was green. Red and green like a holly tree. Why had he only noticed that now? Because he was a self-absorbed workaholic, one who had just had his entire world, his entire existence, turned upside down.

"This is the last stop and it's tricky. Some of the guests might still be up."

"Has anyone ever caught you in the act?"

"Thankfully, no," Holly said. "We all need a little Christmas magic to believe in."

Christmas magic, Nic thought as he opened the van and gathered the last few gifts. Maybe that's what was making him feel lightheaded.

He followed Holly through the snow to the heavily shadowed side of the inn where the door opened directly into the front parlor with its huge, decorated tree. "This way we get in and out fast," she said.

Quickly and quietly, they arranged the gifts they had brought alongside the others beneath the tree. He heard a creak overhead that sounded like it came from the staircase and looked over at Holly, who had heard it as well. Without a word, the two of them scuttled into a nearby alcove, out of sight if anyone came into the room.

Nic looked up. If that wasn't fortuitous. Mistletoe! He pulled Holly into his arms as somewhere on the other side of the house, a clock chimed midnight.

"Merry Christmas," he whispered, his lips an inch from hers. Then he kissed her.

Holly wound her arms around his neck and kissed him back as if her life depended on it. As if she was starving and he was food. Her need fueled his, and he chafed in frustration at the layers of clothing between them. He needed her. Wanted her. All of her. Forever!

He froze. Where had that thought come from? They'd only met yesterday. He couldn't possibly feel this way so quickly. Then his traitorous body betrayed him, convincing him that anything was possible with the magic of Christmas.

* * *

Holly snuck silent, sideways glances at Nico as he drove back to town. Normally she felt elated— another successful Christmas delivery behind her— while Christmas day lay ahead. She got a rush imagining the excitement and joy of the next morning; the small part she played.

Tonight, she just felt confused.

They reached town a short time later, where the soft peal of Christmas bells sent a few stragglers rushing to midnight mass. The carolers had left, but the Commons was still ablaze with lights. The town reverberated with an air of peace and serenity that Holly had always enjoyed as she returned from her rounds. Tonight felt different.

Or was it simply the emotions churning around inside her? The joy of spending Christmas Eve with Nico, coupled with the bleakness of knowing that in less than two days he would return to his life in the city, while her life would never be the same.

It wasn't fair. He'd disrupted her life once, years ago. Now, he was doing it all over again.

As she studied his profile, he turned a soft smile her way, as if he felt her eyes on him.

"I really enjoyed tonight. Thanks for letting me tag along," he said. "Somewhere over the years, I lost sight of the true meaning of Christmas."

Holly froze. He'd said those exact words to her in New York.

* * *

When Nico followed her inside, Holly got the distinct feeling he had no intention of leaving. And suddenly she didn't want him to. Normally, as the rush of elation dissipated, she was left with a drained feeling that came after. But not tonight. Not with the way Nico was looking at her.

"I'll light a fire," he said, going over to the

fireplace and setting up paper and kindling as if he'd been doing it all his life.

"I'll make some tea. Or would you rather have hot chocolate?"

He turned her way, still squatting by the fire, and his expression tugged at something deep inside her. "I'd rather have you."

It took everything in Holly to laugh off his words and limp into the kitchen where she filled the kettle and put it on to boil. Her hands were as unsteady as her heartbeat as she leaned over the sink, schooling herself to get a grip.

Did she want that, too? Did she want Nico for this one night if that was all she could have?

Unsure, but feeling more composed, she turned and blundered straight into him. He dwarfed her small kitchen, just like he had that night in New York.

"Sorry," he said ruefully. "That was a really cheesy thing to say, and I'm not normally that guy."

Holly pushed an unsteady hand through her hair, and stared at the expensive buttons fronting his denim shirt. "I know that."

Neither of them moved, yet the air between them seemed to crackle. She could hear the thud of her heart, pumping blood through her veins. Or was that his heart, beating in tandem with hers?

She watched as Nico moved in slow motion, his hand beneath her chin, tipping her face up to his.

"I'm not sure if it's just the holiday season, but I'm kind of at a loss right now. It's late and I know I ought to go, but something in me is clamoring to stay for as long as you'll have me."

A lifetime, Holly thought. She wanted him to stay for a lifetime.

"I know," she said. "Let's heat up the rest of the pizza."

"Great idea."

And just like that, the mood was broken. Nico stepped back while Holly switched on the oven and made tea, after which Nico helped carry cups and plates through to the living room.

Once there, Holly caught her breath. The fire crackled invitingly. Nico had pulled the couch in front of it, along with the coffee table, and lit her candle display on the mantle.

"I hope you don't mind," he said huskily. "I took a few liberties."

She put the teapot down before she dropped it. "I don't mind at all."

They'd eaten pizza that night in New York, one from her freezer that had been there longer than she remembered and tasted like cardboard, but neither of them had cared. They'd been lost in the moment, lost in each other, and it was happening all over again.

Tonight, the pizza tasted better, and she had a larger home complete with a fireplace and Christmas tree, but until Nico had shown up, something had always been missing. But not anymore. Tonight, everything felt complete.

As they talked, she learned a lot had changed in Nico's life since last time they were together. He had made partner in the firm where he worked, and had prosecuted some high-profile cases that even she had heard about. He didn't mention a girlfriend or a romantic life, and she didn't ask.

"That was good," she said as she reached for her tea; nothing left in the pizza box but crumbs.

"Pizza is always better the second day," Nico said. "Except—" He paused, his gaze directed over her head and off in the distance, as if a distant memory was tugging at him. Holly cleared her throat.

He blinked and came back to her, as with one easy movement, he pulled her close, snuggled against his side. "This is better, too," he said.

Holly couldn't argue.

"How'd you wind up in Dickens?" he asked. "I know Sherry moved here because of her husband's work, and moved our mother with them."

"Would you believe I googled 'best small towns to live in the US?'"

"Get out!"

"I kid you not. My sister lives a few towns over, and I wanted to be close but not that close. I was tired of the anonymity of the big city. Given a name like mine, I've always been drawn to all things Christmas, so this town had me from my first visit. I started off doing some freelance photo work for the paper, then met some of the locals, and eventually hung out my shingle as a photographer."

Nico was looking down at her with admiration. "That is one gutsy move. To just show up and start over. What about what you left behind? Friends or—"

Holly shifted to face him. "I'll always have my memories," she said softly.

"I'm really glad I came," Nico said.

"What took you so long?" Holly asked.

Her words held a double-meaning that he wouldn't recognize. Why did it take him so long to find her?

"I don't even have an excuse," Nico said. Again, his eyes got that faraway look. "I think maybe I was looking in the wrong place for something that didn't exist."

"Would you care to elaborate?" Holly asked.

"Mostly, I didn't want to feel like a third wheel at Sherry's Christmas with her husband," he said lightly.

Third wheel meant there was no girlfriend.

"That wouldn't matter to Sherry. Christmas is all about family."

"So they tell us." He turned a speculative look her way. "Where's yours? Family I mean."

"My sister is with a new beau. My mother is somewhere warm with an old beau—" She chuckled. "I guess I see what you mean."

Nico was nodding knowingly. "See? You didn't want to be a third wheel any more than I did."

"At least I put up a tree," Holly said. "And accepted a dinner invitation from friends. I'm not sitting around alone being Scrooge."

Nico nodded. "Not to mention your Christmas project doing for others. Clearly, you are a far better person than I am."

"I don't know about that," Holly said, smothering a yawn.

"Ever sit up all night talking?" Nico asked abruptly.

"I did once. Why?"

He grinned. "Want to go for two?"

"I think maybe once was enough," Holly said. "We could never recreate that magic."

"That good, huh?"

"The stuff of dreams," Holly murmured, snuggling closer to Nico.

He rested his cheek against the top of her head. "I'll never forget this night."

Yes, you will, Holly thought, just before she fell asleep, cozy and safe in Nico's arms for the second time in her life.

Chapter 8

Nic woke up, his arm beneath Holly asleep, the fire dead in the grate, and the soft gray light of dawn visible through the window. Gently, he disentangled himself from the woman in his arms, rose and stretched.

He had no business feeling so good after a cramped night on Holly's couch, but he truly had had the best sleep he remembered in years. Maybe ever. He looked down at Holly, still sound asleep. Something about the way she slept, curled up like a kitten, niggled at his brain. It all felt so familiar. As if he'd experienced it before somewhere.

He peered into her bedroom and spotted an extra blanket, neatly folded on the end of her bed. He brought it out and quietly draped it over her. She didn't wake, but seemed to snuggle into the warmth.

When he went to use the bathroom he discovered Holly's gallery, where dozens of black and white photos framed in plain black frames took up most of the wall space. There were older pictures, clearly not taken by Holly, showing her with hair so blonde it was almost white. One wall of photos was more recent, and many had her recognizable style.

There were also photos from what looked to be family vacations, Holly and another blonde girl, probably a year or two younger, with an older, fair-haired woman in the middle, likely her mother. There were others of Holly and the second girl, who must be her sister.

Abruptly, he froze! His hand shook as he lifted a photo from the wall and took it over to the window to study it closely. He recognized Holly instantly, her unmistakable smile, the glint of laughter in her eyes, her glossy black hair. Black hair! Not like the blonde tangle of her youth or the softly curling rainbow shade right now, but jet black and straight.

He felt like someone just punched him in the gut. Carefully he replaced the picture on the wall, then he went back to study the still-sleeping Holly. Everything about the night in New York came flooding back to him. The similarities leading up to now. Her tumbling into him with him trying to save her, so they wound up on the ice, tangled in each other's arms.

The easy banter and the effortless conversation between them as they skated together for a while, then went back to her place where they sat up most of the night talking, before eventually falling asleep in each others' arms on her couch after eating frozen pizza.

She'd refused to tell him her name when he left, saying when he found her number and called her, that would be his reward.

"I'm Nico," he'd said. "So you know who I am when I call."

"Oh, I'll know who you are," she'd said in that light-hearted way of hers. "Don't you worry about that. Serendipity will bring us together."

He'd had to look up the meaning of serendipity on his phone. The next day, he'd mailed the Christmas decoration to his mother, and he'd never found her number. At some point in the new year he'd gone around to her apartment, but the door had been answered by a stranger. He'd shrugged it off and carried on with his life, even if he did show up every Christmas Eve at Rockefeller Center, looking for a girl he barely remembered, except the way he felt when he was with her.

Serendipity had a weird sense of humor.

It was all too much for him!

Quietly he shrugged into his coat and let himself out, being careful to lock the door behind him. He hadn't changed much in five years, so she must have known who he was! Why hadn't she said anything?

Maybe he wasn't as unforgettable as he thought.

The cold morning air hit him in the face with an icy blast and cleared away the cobwebs. What was she supposed to say? "Sorry you don't remember me from five years ago when you promised to call and never did." Like, *that* wouldn't have been awkward!

At least he knew why he felt like he'd known

her before. And if serendipity had taken on the form of that silver angel to bring them together—not that he believed in stuff like that.

He started toward Sherry's house. The boys would be up soon, and Sherry could use his help. He stopped abruptly. Holly was coming for dinner and there was nothing from him under the tree for her. He took a hasty detour into town. It was Christmas day, but surely some of the shops would be open for at least a few hours.

His steps slowed as he reached town, aware he wasn't thinking straight. It was the wee hours on Christmas morning, and anyone who was up this early wasn't rushing off to work, they were with their family or on their way to mass. He shoved his bare hands into his coat pockets, no idea where his gloves were. Probably back at Holly's.

What the—!

There must have been a piece of straw or a pine needle in his pocket for something pricked his finger, which he pulled out to stare at the drop of blood instead of watching where he was going.

When he looked up, he was in front of the Gift Emporium. He peered through the window. Too bad it wasn't open. He could buy Holly something cool for her tree. Something to remember him by.

Suddenly, he saw movement from inside the shop. It was that woman, the one Sherry had said used to be an actress. She wasn't in her elf costume today, but dressed like a gypsy or a fortune teller, with layers of scarves and shiny jewelry. Impulsively he banged on the window to get her attention.

She looked up, then slowly made her way to the door.

"Sorry to bother you," Nic said, with his most contrite smile. "I've got a bit of an emergency."

"Come in," she said." I've been expecting you."

Nic started. *Had he heard right?*

"My crystal ball said you would need my help," she said. "What brings you here?"

Crystal ball! Yeah, right.

"I need a gift for someone. I believe you know

84

Holly. Can you help me?"

She gave him a slow, thorough perusal, then led the way through the crowded shop to a bookshelf crammed with children's books.

"Oh, I don't think a book would be the right gift," he said. "I was thinking about something for her tree."

She ignored him and reached up to the top shelf, pulled down a book, then turned to face him. "Don't think. Listen," she said dramatically. "This is a first edition; very rare. I've been keeping it for her, for when the time is right. When her wish came true."

She passed Nic the book, still sporting its original paper dust jacket, faded with time. On the jacket was an old-fashioned scene of a girl in a green coat with a red scarf and red mittens. He flipped it open to the copyright page. 1956. Long before Holly's time.

"The story of Holly and Ivy," the woman said helpfully, as if Nic couldn't read. "It's a book about wishing," she added.

As Nic hesitated, wondering if an old-fashioned kids' story, first edition or not, was a suitable gift, a sharp corner of the dust jacket pricked his finger.

Serendipity was apparently telling him it was. Maybe serendipity only worked if one believed in its power. "I'll take it," he said.

The woman nodded, an approving gleam in her eye.

* * *

The second Holly woke up, she knew Nico was gone. She felt his absence as keenly she'd felt as his presence earlier.

She sighed, rolled over, and pushed herself to her feet. Except this time was different. This time she got to face him the next day.

The second she set foot on the floor, something felt different. She took one experimental step, then a second; flexed one ankle, then the other. Not a twinge. Not the faintest reminder of her injury from the other night. From atop her tiny tree on the other side of the room, the angel swirled merrily even though there was no breeze, as if she knew something Holly didn't.

* * *

Holly climbed the steps to Sherry's porch juggling a poinsettia, a bottle of wine, and a bag of gifts. Begging off tonight hadn't been an option. She'd never let her friend down, and truthfully, she longed to see Nico one last time.

She could do this. Thank him for his help last night, and laugh about falling asleep on him like a bad hostess.

Nico answered the door before she could even knock. He was wearing a gray cashmere sweater that matched his eyes perfectly, and had never looked so tall, dark and desirable. He must have noticed her staring because he laughed.

"I brought an ugly Christmas sweater in case there was a dress code, but I'm off the hook. Here, let me."

He rescued the poinsettia and bottle of wine and ushered her in.

"Sherry's upstairs with the boys on a time out," Nico said. "To say they're a little wound up would be an understatement, and I have to confess I'm largely at fault."

Holly shot him a look. "Aren't you here to help?"

"I thought that meant carve the turkey." His eyes twinkled to let her know he was kidding. "Where should I put this?" He indicated the plant.

"Some place out of danger of three-year-olds' flying feet, I guess."

He set the plant on top of an old-fashioned writing desk and turned to face her. "It should be safe there."

Holly took off her coat, hat, and gloves, unwound her scarf from her neck, and laid everything across the back of an armchair. "How was Christmas morning?"

"Bedlam," Nico said, then grinned. "Sherry didn't expect to have three little boys on her hands, but it was the most fun I've had in years." He paused. "Except for last night. That was really special. How's the ankle?"

"Good as new. And thank you for your help

last night. It was very appreciated."

He continued to look at her in an unsettling way. "Happy to have been of service." He looked down at the bottle of wine in his hand. "I'll go put this in the fridge."

"It's red," Holly said.

"Oh, right." He recovered quickly. "Do we need a decanter?"

"It's not that good of a vintage," Holly said. "Just open it and put it on the table for dinner."

Minutes later, Sherry came down the stairs with two unnaturally quiet little boys, each holding one of her hands.

"Something smells awesome," Holly said.

"I love turkey," Sherry said. "It makes the whole house smell like a holiday." When she reached the bottom of the steps and released the boys, they broke ranks and ran to Holly.

"Did you bring us presenth?" Robbie lisped.

"Didn't I tell you it wasn't polite to ask?" Sherry said.

"You told us if we didn't listen, that Santa

would take back our stuff," said Will.

Holly approached the tree and picked up the gifts she had placed there. As she straightened, a piece of wire from one of the gifts' ribbons pricked her finger. Before she passed the gifts to Sherry and the boys, she looked up and saw writing on the underside of a shiny red Christmas ball; her old phone number.

She blinked and looked again. What was Nico's Christmas decoration doing on Sherry's tree?

She glanced across to the fireplace where Nico stood watching her, and shrugged off the eerie feeling that he knew exactly what she was thinking. Holly cleared her throat.

"Go ahead and open them," she said to the boys who ripped enthusiastically into their gifts as if it was the only one they had received in months.

"Cool!" they said in unison.

"They're for the tree," Holly said, in case there was any question. She had bought them each a wooden ornament realistically fashioned like a musical instrument, a drum for Will and a trumpet for Robbie.

"They match," Will said. "Uncle Nic got us stuff for the tree too." He pointed out his wooden soldier with the drum.

"Great minds think alike," Nic said quietly, still watching Holly in that unsettling way. Something inside her kicked into gear. If she didn't know he didn't remember her, she would almost think—

"This is from me." Sherry handed her a package wrapped in paper decorated with red and green holly. "We can open them together."

"And this is from me." Nico handed her a compact flat package, also wrapped in holly-themed paper.

"I didn't get you anything," she said awkwardly.

"Good," Nico said. "Because you've already given me something priceless. An unforgettable Christmas Eve."

"Earth to Holly," Sherry said as she tugged on the ribbons adorning her gift. "I'm starting without you."

Conscious of Nico's gaze on her, Holly found it nearly impossible to concentrate as she opened her gift from Sherry, and peeled back the paper to reveal a decorative wooden plaque. It was painted with a branch of holly with a shiny wishing star above. The message was simple. *May all your wishes come true*.

"Holly's superstitious about wishes," Sherry told Nico as she finished unwrapping a ceramic teapot in the shape of a fancy high-heeled shoe. She squealed in delight. "I love it!" She turned to Nico. "Holly knows I love all things shoes, even ones I can't wear."

Nico was still watching Holly. "One more to go," he said.

"It feels like a book." Holly untied the ribbon and loosened the tape holding each corner. She hoped it was a book. Something impersonal like a new bestseller.

As she tore away the paper, her hands started to shake. Her eyes filled with tears. She glanced up at

Nico in shock. "I—I—" Words were impossible.

Sherry glanced over her shoulder. "*The Story of Holly and Ivy*." She laughed. "Is that a story about you and your sister?"

Holly smoothed the paper dustjacket reverently. "My sister, Ivy, and I were given this book when we were young. Every night for the entire week before Christmas, our mother would read it to us in installments. We each printed our name in the front in misshapen, grade school letters. Even after we were old enough to read it for ourselves, our mother carried on the tradition. We'd sit in front of the fire and listen as she read, right up until the year she moved away. After we had our own places, Ivy and I used to pass it back and forth every Christmas so we could take turns reading it. One year, Ivy lost it when she moved."

She glanced up at Nico who was watching her in a warm, caring way that churned up her insides. How did he know?

"Wow!" Sherry rose. "Hit that one out of the ballpark, big brother."

Nico shrugged modestly. "I figured anyone who lives on Holly and Ivy Lane would appreciate the story."

"What'th it about, Holly?" asked Robbie.

"It's a story about wishing. Every time in the story, when someone gets pricked, they're supposed to make a wish."

Robbie's face wrinkled. "Why would they do that?"

"It's to remind people to never stop wishing." She glanced back at Nico. "This is a first edition."

"Sherry collects teapots. I happened to notice you collect books."

Woodenly, Holly found her way to her feet and crossed what felt like an immense chasm between herself and Nico. When she reached his side, she froze. She wanted to hug him. But something held her back.

She needed to tell him they'd met before. Show him the decoration. They could laugh about the coincidence. She cleared her throat. "It was a wonderful gift. Thank you."

With one fluid move from Nico, Holly found herself in his arms. "Merry Christmas, Holly, my Christmas girl. I hope you don't mind that I read the book before I wrapped it."

As she put her arms around him, she brushed a piece of holly on the mantle behind him, and pulled her hand away slowly. She didn't need any more reminders to never stop wishing.

"Come on boys," Sherry said, behind her. "Come and help me get the snacks."

"There's something I have to tell you," Holly said to Nico, as the trio trooped from the room. "I should have told you right away."

"You mean this not being our first, but our second Christmas Eve together?"

She started. "You knew?"

"Not at first, but I figured it out eventually. The girl who wouldn't give me her name." His hold tightened around her waist. "You know the real reason I never came to Sherry's before at Christmas?"

Holly shook her head.

"Every Christmas Eve I went to Rockefeller Center, hoping against hope to see you there. That we could recreate the magic of our first meeting."

A massive lump formed in Holly's throat.

"When I couldn't find your number, I went around to your apartment but you'd moved by then."

Holly swallowed thickly. "My schooling was finished," she said. "That's when I moved here."

"I found your number a few days ago when Sherry and I were decorating the tree."

"I thought I was so smart writing it on the ball," Holly said. "That you'd go home and see my number when you hung the ball on your tree."

"Instead, I wrapped it and mailed my mother her late Christmas gift."

"And found my number at this late date," Holly said, as she raised her mouth for his kiss. "Serendipity at last."

"Better late than never," Nico said, as he sealed their future with a promise of much more to come.

Eventually the kiss ended, but Holly remained

safe in the circle of Nico's arms, her head on his shoulder, her hand resting comfortably on his chest.

"Hey!" Sherry arrived from the kitchen. "I've got a turkey that needs carving, a table that needs setting, and two little boys who want to go skating after dinner."

Nico smiled down at Holly. "Holly and I love ice skating."

"As long as no one knocks me over."

"I'll always be there to break your fall."

This time she believed him.

A few hours later, full of turkey and giddy with happiness, Holly and Nico were gliding hand in hand across the ice at Gridley's pond on the edge of town. Sherry and the boys flew by them in the opposite direction, waving vigorously.

"I didn't know the twins could skate so well," Holly said.

"I sent them skates last year for Christmas," Nico said. "Maybe one Christmas Eve they'll meet the woman of their dreams, the same way I met mine."

DEAR READER

Whether you believe in serendipity or not, I hope you enjoyed Holly and Nico's story. We all need a little bit of Christmas Magic. Here's wishing you and your family a wonderful, magical holiday season.

I enjoy reading all types of books as long as there is a happy ending. This lifelong wide range of reading has greatly influenced my own writing interests. Historical or contemporary, steamy or sweet, suspenseful or not, I have a lot more stories to tell.

I hope you find something among my varied offerings to match your tastes and enhance your reader enjoyment. When you do, please brighten my day by leaving a short reader review on the platform of your choice. A line or two saying why you liked the book will help other readers with their choices.

Please review *Holly's Wish* wherever you purchased it or on Goodreads or BookBub.

Note: My steamy titles are very sexually explicit, and not for everyone.

Turn the page to read an excerpt from *No Groom at the Inn.*

NO GROOM AT THE INN

Excerpt Copyright © 2021 Kathleen Lawless

Meredith rose just as the GM's secretary poked her head in the door. "Mer, when you're done, there's someone here to see you."

Probably Bridezilla. "Tell whoever it is I'll be right out."

Asher paused next to her. "Try not to take it so seriously."

"Be more like you, you mean? I'm the wrong gender to be pouring on the charm to the guests the way you do."

Asher gave her his trademark drop-dead gorgeous smile that sent women of all ages into a swoon. "Can I help it if everyone finds me irresistible?"

Meredith arched her brow in acknowledgement. She'd love to hate him, but every word was the truth. He'd started work here the same day she had, and they'd been buddies ever since. Like it or not, he was someone she'd come to rely on.

"Why don't you come with me?" Meredith said. "Maybe all Bridezilla needs is a reassuring pat on the head and your famous smile."

"You know you can count on me," he said, one arm resting on her hip in that familiar, friendly way he had with everyone, resort staff and guests of all ages.

When they reached the main reception area, Meredith froze.

"What is it?" Asher asked, just as a chorus of voices yelled "Surprise!"

"*Omg!*" Meredith turned to Asher in dismay. "My family! What is everyone doing here?" she said as they converged on her and Asher, everyone talking at once.

"Since you never make it home for Christmas, we decided to come to you." Her mother reached her first and hugged her, her smile widening as she transferred her attention to Asher. "And *this* must be Asher!" She threw her arms around him. Over her mother's head Asher gave her a puzzled look as he returned the hug.

"Nice to meet you, Mrs. Robb."

"Oh, silly boy. So formal. I insist you call me, Helen." She pinched his cheek as if he was a youngster. "You're even more handsome than in your pictures."

Meredith pressed her lips tightly together, and tried to ignore the amused glint in Asher's turquoise eyes.

"You didn't tell me you sent your mom pictures."

"I have to hand it to you two. Such discretion. No one I spoke to had any idea you two were dating, let alone getting engaged."

"Mom, I—"

"Oops," Helen pressed her fingers to her lips. "I know it's not official yet, but you did imply—"

"What did Meredith imply?" Asher asked with mock innocence.

* * *

ALSO BY KATHLEEN LAWLESS

Sweet Western Historical Romance
THE SPINSTER TAKES A GROOM SERIES
The Gambler
The Magician

Western Historical Romance
Grace's Folly
Anora's Pride
Callie's Honor
Maddy's Fugitive
Widows, Babies and Brides (Box Set of all 4)

Sweet Western Historical Romance
SEVEN BRIDES FOR SEVEN BROTHERS
SERIES
Brody's Bride - Book 1
Bradley's Bride - Book 2
Braydon's Bride - Book 3
Blake's Bride - Book 4
Bishop's Bride - Book 5
Barron's Bride - Book 6
Benjamin's Bride - Book 7
Seven Brides for Seven Brothers Box Set 1 -
Prequel & Books 1 to 3
Seven Brides for Seven Brothers Box Set 2 - Books
4 to 7

Sweet Western Historical Romance
WIDOWS OF THE WILD WEST
Hope
Janie
Sweet Western Historical Romance
MAIL ORDER BRIDES
Mail Order Olivia
Mail Order Rachel
Mail Order Martina
A Bride for Shane
A Bride for Riley
A Bride for Weston
Mail Order Noelle
Chelsea's Choice
Lila: Rescue Me Mail Order Brides
Here Come the Brides Volume 1
Here Come the Brides Volume 2

Sweet Contemporary Romance
Frannie (Always a Bridesmaid)
Baxter (Last Man Standing)
Blue Sky Island
One Cinderella Spring
One Stolen Summer
One Fantasy Fall
One Wondrous Winter

Sweet Christmas Romance Novellas
Holly's Wish
No Groom at the Inn

Women's Fiction
Fabulous at Fifty

Romantic Suspense
Final Heat
Afterburn

Steamy Historical Romance
Taboo
Unmasked
Reckless Rogues - Box Set of the 2 Books

Steamy Contemporary Romance
SECRET SEDUCTIONS
Her Untamed Cowboy - Book 1
Her Undercover Cowboy - Book 2
Her Unwilling Cowboy - Book 3
Who Needs a Cowboy! - Book 4
Intimate Strangers

* * *

For a complete book list visit *KathleenLawless.com*
To be the first to hear about Kathleen's new releases, special fan pricing sales, and also receive a free book, sign up for her VIP Reader Newsletter. You can find the sign-up link on her website.

ABOUT THE AUTHOR

USA Today Bestselling Author Kathleen Lawless blames a misspent youth watching Rawhide, Maverick and Bonanza for her fascination with cowboys, which doesn't stop her from creating a wide variety of interests and occupations for her many alpha male heroes.

With over 50 published novels to her credit, she enjoys pushing the boundaries of traditional romance into historical romance, contemporary romance, romantic suspense and women's fiction.

She makes her home in the Pacific Northwest and loves to hear from her readers.

* * *

Find Kathleen on her website: *KathleenLawless.com* and on *Goodreads, BookBub, Facebook, Instagram*, and *TikTok*.

.